BRAINJUICE
AMERICAN HISTORY
fresh squeezed!

41 thirst-for-knowledge–quenching poems by
CAROL DIGGORY SHIELDS

illustrations by
RICHARD THOMPSON

HANDPRINT BOOKS ✋ BROOKLYN, NEW YORK

To Christopher, Ann, Gina, Paula, and Todd
—C.D.S.

For Emma now and Charlotte later
—R.T.

Text copyright © 2002 by Carol Diggory Shields
Illustrations copyright © 2002 by Richard Thompson
Cover and interior design by Karen Kane and Todd Sutherland
All rights reserved

Library of Congress Cataloging-in-Publication Data

Shields, Carol Diggory.
 American history, fresh squeezed!: 41 thirst-for-knowledge-quenching poems / by
Carol Diggory Shields ; enriched with illustrations by Richard Thompson.-- 1st ed.
  p. cm. -- (BrainJuice)
 Includes index.
 Summary: A collection of poems on such important events in the history of the United
States as the Pilgrims' landing in Massachusetts, the Louisiana Purchase, the Civil War,
Seward's Folly, the San Francisco earthquake, and more.
  ISBN 1-929766-62-9
 1. United States--History--Juvenile Poetry. 2. Children's Poetry, American. [1. United
States--History--Poetry. 2. American poetry.] I. Thompson, Richard, 1957-ill. II. Title.

PS3569.H48328 A824 2002
811'.54--dc2   2002027594

All trademark names in this text are the property of their respective owners
BrainJuice is a registered trademark of Handprint Books

First published in hardcover in the United States in 2003 by Handprint Books
413 Sixth Avenue
Brooklyn, New York 11215
www.handprintbooks.com

Hardcover First Edition
ISBN: 1-929766-62-9
2 4 6 8 10 9 7 5 3

Paperback edition first published in 2005
ISBN: 1-59354-120-1
2 4 6 8 10 9 7 5 3 1

Printed in China

Dear Miss Tibbits:

I was probably the worst student you ever had in all your years of teaching sixth-grade history at North Shore Middle School. I was convinced history was just a lot of boring dates and wars, and tried my best to get the class to agree. Remember the ladybug races? The water balloons?

This is an apology. Not so much for the balloons and the bugs, but for a really rotten attitude. I grew up. I became a poet (believe it or not!). And I learned that history is stories. Stories about people—scared people doing brave things, smart people doing stupid things, people setting off on journeys to unknown destinations, and people risking their lives to help people they'd never even met. There are more interesting, inspiring, funny, and yes, depressing and disgusting stories in American history than I could ever write poems about, but I decided to try. I wanted to write about the times and the people that would have spoken to me, had I been paying attention back in sixth grade. No doubt I have left out a number of really important stories—I know I can count on you to tell me what they are.

And Miss Tibbits, I have done one more thing you may not like: I shortened everything. Why can't you learn about the Boston Tea Party in 17 lines? Or the Louisiana Purchase in 10? Oh dear, I can just hear you sigh. But I have made progress, haven't I?

With fond memories, apologies,
best wishes, and thanks,

Your former student,
Carol Diggory Shields

**Dinosaurs
walk on Earth**
|
245,000,000 B.C.

**Extinction of
the dinosaurs,
large mammals appear**
|
65,000,000 B.C.

The First

The first Americans who roamed the prairie
Were kind of big and kind of scary.
Some lived alone, some in a bunch,
A few of them ate the others for lunch.
Some were gentle, some were mean,
Some were spotted or dotted or green.
They hissed and growled and roared great roars—
The first Americans were dinosaurs.

Discovery

In fourteen hundred ninety-two,
Columbus did not have a clue;
He sailed to the west, bumped into land:
"Hooray—it's India . . . unless it's Japan,
So I'll call the people Indian folk!"
(The natives thought he was making a joke.)

Next came Vespucci, called Amerigo,
A little bit smarter, he said, "I know,
This is a new place, and with all modesty,
I think we should name it after me."
So with his first name the New World got stuck,
But it could have been worse—

                    he might have been Chuck.

First permanent English
colony is founded at
Jamestown, called "Jimtown"
|
1607

English colonists prepare
to leave Jimtown
|
1609

Colonists decide to stay
following first
tobacco harvest

1611

Before going ashore, Pilgrims
check to see how they look, using
the Mayflower Compact

1620

The Pilgrims

The Pilgrims were grumpy, their clothing was frumpy;
The English king said, "Go away!
To some new location or some other nation,
Where you can pray any old way."

They hired a boat, for weeks they did float
Without a bathroom or even a shower,
No toilet, no tub, no sink for a scrub
(It didn't smell like a mayflower).

The Pilgrims all cheered when land soon appeared,
The captain said, "Wrong place, I fear."
There wasn't a dock, they jumped off on a rock,
"Forget it, we're staying right here!"

**Dutchman Peter Minuit buys Manhattan Island from local Indians.
He thinks they own the land (they don't).**

1626

Manhattan

From the Carnarsie Indians, the clever Dutch
Bought some land for not very much.
24 dollars for Manhattan isle!
The Dutchmen signed on the line with a smile,
What a bargain! What a deal!
(You might even say it was a steal.)
But the Dutchmen failed to understand,
That the Carnarsie tribe didn't own the land.

Christmas is declared illegal
in Massachusetts Bay Colony

1659

Tea is introduced into
the American colonies

1714

The first American public library
is founded by Benjamin Franklin
(library card, please!)

1731

The first umbrella used in
Windsor, Connecticut, produces
"a riot of merriment and derision"

1740

Recipe

Water (1 harborful),
Sailing ships (3),
1 very dark night,
300 crates tea.
96 colonists
(Mad about taxes,
Dressed up as Indians,
Carrying axes).

British government imposes the Sugar Act, Quartering Act, Currency Act, Townshend Act, Coercive Act, Stamp Act, and Tea Act

1764-73

Boston Tea Party— Revolutionary War is brewing

December 16, 1773

Using the axes,
Smash up the tea,
Dump overboard,
Stir vigorously.
Add some of the crates,
Let brew for a while,

Result?

    1 Tea Party,

    Boston-style.

Explanation

The colonists said, "Tarnation!
We're sick of this aggravation,
Tyranny, taxes, and tariffs—
We want a separation!"

Without further hesitation,
They wrote a brave declaration,
Stating complete independence
From the bossy British nation.

"Egad—what an irritation!"
Sighed the king in exasperation.
(George III didn't understand
The rebels' determination.)

They faced poverty and starvation,
A hopeless situation,
But the ragtag Yankee rebels
Won a hard-fought liberation.

Which is why on our vacation,
We set off a conflagration
With flaming franks and fireworks,
Our Fourth of July celebration!

Thomas Jefferson builds dome on
Monticello to hide billiards room;
game is illegal

A submarine is developed by
Robert Fulton; the government
doesn't see any use for it

1800

1800

First comic magazine,
The Wasp, **is published**

The U.S. purchases the
Louisiana Territory from France—
800,000 sq. miles for $15,000,000.01

1801

1803

The Purchase

Tom Jefferson went shopping for a city, one fine day,
Something in the South, with a harbor or a bay.
"Voila!" said the French, "the city of your dreams!
For only 15 million, we will sell you New Orleans."
"It's very nice," said Tom, "but that's quite a lot to pay."
"Mais non! Not when you hear about our special of the day—
We'll add the Rocky Mountains, the Mississippi shore,
The Great Plains and the bayous, for only one cent more!"
We'll never fill up that much land, thought Tom,
    but what the heck,
"We'll buy it all," he said at last. "Will you take a check?"

**President Jefferson appoints
Lewis and Clark to explore the area
acquired in the Louisiana Purchase**

1803

Job Available

Opening for a teenage girl
(With baby in a pack):
Help lead an expedition
Twelve hundred miles and back,
Translate several languages,
Assist with navigation,
Swim freezing rivers, climb high peaks,
Save group from near-starvation.
Help make peace with hostile tribes,
Work both night and day *

* No vacation, health insurance, benefits, or pay.

Lewis and Clark hire a French-Canadian fur trader as an interpreter; his Shoshone wife, Sacajawea, is far more helpful

1804

**THIRD CENSUS: U.S. population reaches
7.2 million, including 1.4 million African-
Americans—1.2 million of whom are slaves**

1810

*Please rise and sing the following poem
to the tune of "The Star-Spangled Banner,"
preferably in three-part harmony.*

To the Tune of...

Oh, say can you see, Mr. Francis Scott Key,
Held hostage on board, to keep him out of trouble
As big British ships, sailing in from the sea
Were trying to bomb, Fort McHenry to rubble.
And as he caught sight, in the dawn's early light,
Of the flag waving there, Francis started to write.
A song that was brave, bold, and in-spir-ing—
Sadly set to a tune, that nobody can sing.

Under the Indian Removal Act, various southeastern tribes are moved to the west. Thousands die on the journey, and none was repaid for land, homes, and goods taken.

1816-1858

Trail of Tears

Have you seen the Cherokee?
Lovers of their land, teachers of their children,
They learned the secrets of the written words,
They danced the Eagle Dance.

    We have seen them.
    They passed this way, going west.
    Carrying all they owned, in their arms and on their backs.
    They have not returned.

Construction begins on the Erie Canal, which will connect the Great Lakes and Ohio and Mississippi valleys with the Hudson River and Atlantic Ocean

1817

Have you seen the Choctaw?
Children of Nanih Waiya, the sacred mound,
Singers and poets, planters and harvesters,
They would let no person go hungry.

> We have seen them.
> They passed this way, going west.
> Their old ones were dying, their children cried out.
> They have not returned.

Have you seen the Creek?
Dwellers on the riverbanks, tall and strong,
Ruled by the Beloved Men,
Celebrating the days of the Green Corn.

We have seen them.
They passed this way, going west.
Their food was almost gone, and they had no more.
They have not returned.

Have you seen the Chickasaw?
Fierce in games and fierce in war,
Proud and tattooed, quick to fight,
Fishers of Mississippi waters.

> We have seen them.
> They passed this way, going west.
> Their feet were bare, and they had no blankets.

> > They have not returned.

PRESIDENTS ON PARADE
1789 Part I 1845

The presidents are passing by—Stand up and holler!

Number one is Washington,
His picture's on the dollar.
John Adams is next in line,
A smart but grumpy fellow,
Third is Thomas Jefferson,
Builder of Monticello.
Madison is fourth, but first
To call the White House home,
Monroe's doctrine declared:
"Hands off! Leave us alone!"

Adams II was grumpy,
A lot like dear old pop,
Jackson was a country boy
As skinny as a mop.
Van Buren, called "The Fox,"
Was clever, smooth, and slick.
Harrison, at his own parade,
Got sick and died quite quick.
Veep John Tyler took over,
Handsome, tall, and lean,
He must have liked kids a lot,
'Cause he had about fifteen.

Baseball

It started with a sunny day,
A stick, a ball, a place to play.
A grassy lawn, guys hanging out,
A pitch, crrr-aack, a hit, a shout.
Bases marked with stones or sticks,
"You go first; we'll get last licks."
Then came rules and teams and parks,
Uniforms, lights for the dark,
Leagues and owners, honors, shame,
Heroes, records, scandals, fame.
And still it starts with a sunny day,
A stick and a ball and a place to play.

The Oregon Trail stretches 2,000 miles from Missouri to the Pacific coast. Over 500,000 people make the 5-month journey to the West.

1840s-1860s

Mormons arrive in Utah and found Deseret

1847

Vehicle

Slightly used, all-terrain SUV,
Model year 1843.
Four-oxen drive, convertible roof,
Guaranteed rain- and arrow-proof.

Uncomfortably seats a family of four,
Including furniture, chickens, and more.
Top speed: 50 miles per week
(Faster careening down from a peak).

Gold is discovered
in California

1848

Harriet Beecher Stowe
publishes
Uncle Tom's Cabin

1852

Blue jeans are
invented by
Levi Strauss

1853

Music system in stereo,
Fiddle, harmonica, one old banjo.
Four sturdy tires of wood and steel
For that bouncy off-road feel.

Driven to Oregon (just one way),
Make an offer and take it away!

The Underground Railroad is a secret
network of routes to help slaves escape
to Canada, where they could live in freedom

1830-1865

Massachusetts
declares
Christmas lega

1856

This Train

The passengers are hidden,
The conductors are on guard.
The stations secret places—
A cellar, a barn, a yard.
The train tracks are invisible,
Hope is the engineer,
The final stop is freedom
From slavery and fear.

Confederates open fire on Fort
Sumter in Charleston, South
Carolina, beginning the Civil War

Emancipation Proclamation
is issued

April 12, 1861

1863

Civil War

Harper's Ferry,
Shiloh,
Picket's Mill,
Seven Pines,
Appomattox,
Malvern Hill.
Vicksburg,
Atlanta,
Battle of Bull Run.
Names like the beat
Of a muffled drum.

President Lincoln is assassinated;
Lee surrenders the Confederate Army to Grant;
the Thirteenth Amendment abolishes slavery

1865

Cedar Mountain,
Mossy Creek,
Bloody Bridge,
Nashville,
Saltville,
Indian Ridge.
Chickamauga,
Tupelo,
Gettysburg.
Their names are the words
Of a funeral dirge.

Face to face,
Side by side,
We fought ourselves.
Many of us died.

Mr. Seward's Folly

Alaska? I ask ya, who wants such a place?
So cold it freezes the nose off your face.
Tons of ice and miles of snow,
A place where no one wants to go.
What's that you say? It might have gold?
Quick, Mr. Seward, mark it "SOLD!"

The U.S. becomes
the world's foremost
industrial nation

1870-1900

Record number of immigrants
(some 9 million) arrive
in the U.S.

1880-1900

Revolution

It started with Eli's cotton gin
That made cotton easy to pick and spin,
Then the jenny spun thread, clickity-clack,
And the weaving loom shuttled forward and back,
The mill wheels whirled, thumped, and whined,
Turning out goods of every kind.
It grew and grew, an enormous need—
"Give us more power! Give us more speed!"
Huffing and chuffing, engines of steam,
Billows of smoke and whistles that scream,
Riverboats, steamboats, great iron trains,
Churning upriver, chugging through plains.
Faster and faster—no turning back,
Change came barreling down the track.

PRESIDENTS ON PARADE
1845 Part II 1889

Here comes Polk, number eleven,
Added land all kinds of ways,
Followed by Zachary Taylor,
Our chief for five hundred days.
Number thirteen was Fillmore,
Sent the Navy to Japan,
Next was "Handsome Frank,"
Mr. Pierce, a good-looking man.
Along came James Buchanan,
Looked around and said, "Uh-oh!
The Civil War is brewing,
I think I'd better go!"
So Lincoln, Honest Abe,
Faced a troubled nation,

Andrew Johnson	Ulysses S. Grant	Rutherford B. Hayes	James A. Garfield	Chester A. Arthur	Grover Cleveland
1865-1869	1869-1877	1877-1881	1881	1881-1885	1885-1889

Freed slaves throughout the land,
With his Proclamation.
Seventeen, Andrew Johnson,
Got himself impeached,
Ulysses Grant was very shy,
And never gave a speech.
Hayes married "Lemonade Lucy,"
Garfield was shot and died,
Next came "Elegant Arthur,"
His whiskers were his greatest pride.
Then came Grover Cleveland,
Who returned for an encore,
He was president twenty-two,
And also twenty-four.

Teddy

The President said, "Beware!
I'm out to bag a bear."
His guide said, "Over there!
I see one in his lair."
Said Roosevelt, "I declare,
That's just a baby bear—
Hunting it would be unfair!"
The news spread from here to there
That Teddy had spared a bear,
Which is in your bed upstairs,
In cribs, on sofas, in chairs,
Or almost anywhere
You will find a teddy bear.

Poor You

Oh poor, poor you!

All that homework you must do,
And then there are the chores—
Feed the dog, sweep the floors.
Don't you wish that you
Lived in nineteen-oh-two?

Only three short months in school!
(Now that sounds really cool),
And throughout the other nine,
You'd be working in a mine,
Thirteen hours every day
(No summers off
    or time for play).

Or maybe you'd rather chill
By working in a mill,
Tending a huge machine
That spits dirt and grease and steam.
Dawn to dark, rain or shine,
Each day you'd earn one thin dime!

Don't you wish that you
Lived in nineteen-oh-two?

The first piloted, powered
machine achieves flight at
Kitty Hawk, North Carolina

1903

At the World's Fair in St. Louis,
Missouri, Thomas Edison presents
a 7-acre "Palace of Electricity"

1904

Kitty Hawk

There once were two brothers—crazy guys,
Who wished that people could fly,
    Folks said, "By cracky,
    Those Wright boys are wacky,"
Till they looked up and saw them fly by.

San Francisco, 1906

Under the earth, a sleeping giant lies,
Over him, people, as busy as ants,
Built houses, roads, bridges, and towers.
Until one day the giant turned,
And twitched in his sleep,
Shrugged off the houses, bridges, roads, and towers,
And turning again, went back to sleep.
While, busy as ants, the people started building
Houses, roads, bridges, and towers.

The Great War

The First World War,
War of stinking trenches, endless mud,
Ceaseless boom of cannon, the rockets' scream,
Clanking tanks and droning planes,
The rattle of machine-gun fire.

And then in the eleventh month,

On the eleventh day,

At the eleventh hour,

Silence.

Peace.

The Eighteenth Amendment
to the Constitution prohibits
liquor in the U.S.

1919

The Nineteenth Amendment
to the Constitution gives
women the right to vote

1920

Women Get the Vote!

The Declaration writers goofed—
All men created equal?
A hundred and forty years went by
Till they fixed it with a sequel.

There would have been a lot less fuss,
No strife, no fights, no dramas,
If the founding fathers had listened
To the founding mamas.

A Pennsylvania law requires
skirts to be at least four
inches below the knee

1921

Lindbergh flies nonstop
across Atlantic in
Spirit of St. Louis

1927

The Roaring Twenties

In the twenties, guys were dapper,
A girl who was wild was called a flapper.
Girls so wild, that, oh my dears,
They cut their hair up to their ears!
Still more shocking, oh my stars,
Some of them drove motorcars,
Wore skirts so short that, golly gees,
You could almost see their knees!
Put on powder, lipstick too,
Said things like, "Twenty-three, skiddoo!"
It's a good thing, I must say,
That girls don't act like that today.

Prohibition

Prohibition—not a great idea,
It didn't stop people from drinking beer,
They just brewed up their own at home,
Or bought it from bad guys like Al Capone.

Depressing Depression

Money gone, jobs were scarce,
Banks were repossessing,
The Great Depression, all in all,
Was pretty darn depressing.

Franklin Delano Roosevelt is
inaugurated as president

|

1933

The most flouted law in history,
Prohibition, is repealed

|

1933

FDR's ABC

FDR, down in DC,
Said, "We'll end this depression, ASAP.
The CCC and the WPA
Will give folks jobs right away,
While the SSA and the SEC
Will fix the broken economy.
There's the AAA for the farmer's hay,
Electric power from the REA,
With the TVA and PWA,
Soon the USA will be A-OK."

Roosevelt promises a "New Deal,"
numerous programs—referred to by their
initials—to stimulate the economy

1933-1939

Radio drama of H.G. Wells'
War of the Worlds
causes national panic

1938

PRESIDENTS ON PARADE
1889 Part III 1945

Hooray for Harrison, twenty-three,
(His granddad was number nine),
Poor McKinley, twenty-five,
Was killed shaking hands in a line.
Next came Teddy Roosevelt,
(Famous for the bears),
With a bunch of kids who slid
Down the White House stairs.
Taft, twenty-seven,
A big man—super-size.

Woodrow Wilson	Warren G. Harding	Calvin Coolidge	Herbert C. Hoover	Franklin D. Roosevelt
1913-1921	1921-1923	1923-1929	1929-1933	1933-1945

Wilson was a scholar,
And won the Nobel Prize.
Harding and pals played poker,
Carousing through the night,
Next, tall "Silent Cal" Coolidge,
Kept his lips buttoned tight.
Herbert Hoover, thirty-one,
The Depression brought him grief,
Next FDR came along,
His New Deal spelled relief.

The Japanese bomb Pearl Harbor. U.S.
declares war on Germany and Japan
in the days that follow.

Victory in Europe,
"V-E Day"

| December 7, 1941 | May 8, 1945 |

World War II

In our very own galaxy, not long ago,
An evil empire began to grow.
Hitler, Tojo, Mussolini,
Each worse than a movie meanie,
Three dictators with a single goal:
"We want the world under our control!"
But they were defeated, not by computers,
Spaceships, or intergalactic shooters,
Or robot weapons or laser spears,
But by men and women,
    and their blood, sweat, and tears.

The U.S. drops atomic bombs on
the Japanese cities
of Hiroshima and Nagasaki

August 6 and 9, 1945

Victory over Japan,
"V-J Day"

September 2, 1945

◄ **59** ►

The world's first
electronic digital computer
is developed

1946

All New ENIAC!

Be the first one on your block,
Get a computer for your home!
30 tons of lights and buttons,
Wires, tubes, and chrome.
It'll balance your family budget,
Help you do your math,
Solve complicated problems
In an hour and a half!
Buy the ENIAC computer!
Though it's bigger than your house,
Just move into the backyard,
With your children, pets, and spouse.

**Jukeboxes go into
mass production**

**Roswell incident
(supposed alien landing in New Mexi**

|
1946

|
1947

Fun in the Forties

Hooray for Saturday night—
We get to stay up late,
Race through dinner, clean up quick,
"Hurry kids, the program won't wait!"
Mom on the sofa, Dad in his chair,
Only one minute to go—
Until, at last, Dad leans over
And turns on the radio!

Bomb shelter plans become
widely available in
government pamphlets   The Korean War   Diet soda
is introduced

1950s   1950-1953   1952

Fun in the Fifties

The year is 1952,
Television is very new,
A picture the size of a goldfish bowl,
That ripples, zigzags, flips, and rolls.
No satellite dishes—just rabbit ears,
Sometimes a show just disappears.
Wow! Three channels to choose at night,
Broadcast in glorious black-and-white.
Snow and static and "ghosts" on the screen—
The coolest thing we'd ever seen.

Please sit on the floor to sing the following poem to the tune of "The Wheels on the Bus," preferably using appropriate hand gestures.

The Wheels on the (Montgomery) Bus

The driver on the bus said, "Move on back!
Move on back, move on back!
White folk in front and black in back,
All through the town."

Rosa L. Parks said, "I won't move,
I won't move, I won't move.
I'll stay right here
    where I sat down,
All through the town."

**The Supreme Court declares that
Alabama's state and local laws requiring
segregation on buses are illegal**

1956

The policemen said, "You're under arrest,
Under arrest, under arrest."
The policemen said, "You're under arrest,
We're taking you downtown."

The people all said, "Don't ride the bus,
Make a peaceful fuss, but don't ride the bus.
We'll carpool, bike, or walk if we must,
All through the town."

One year later . . .

The people on the bus sit wherever they like,
Wherever they like, wherever they like.
Black and tan and brown and white,
All through the town.

Cold War

There once was a war nobody lost,
A war that nobody won.
Don't know just when it started,
Or just when it was done.
But in a war with Russia,
Against the USA,
I'd rather have a cold war
Than a hot one, any day.

The Soviet Union launches *Sputnik* I
and *Sputnik* II, the beginning
of the "space race"

|

1957

U.S. postal rates go up;
a first-class stamp
costs four cents

|

1958

Space Race

It's the U.S. and Russia in a race for space,
Russia sends up Sputnik, grabs first place.
Then two more Sputniks—
    Russia is sizzling!
The U.S. rockets are all just fizzling.
At last we launch a satellite,
But Russia's ahead with a
    manned space flight!

The Mercury Seven step up to bat,
It's neck and neck, and tit for tat.
Russia goes to the moon and circles around,
Then the U.S. scores big—Apollo touchdown!
We still could be racing to this very day,
But we finally discovered a much better way,
Exploring together the last frontier,
Side by side on the space station MIR.

Dangerous

The grown-ups said, "Oh no, no, no!
This stuff is very bad!
It will warp your mind and make you deaf
And surely drive you mad."
They panned it and they banned it,
Kids listened anyway.
In spite of all the warnings,
Rock 'n' roll was here to stay.

Groovy

I'm looking so groovy
In this patched denim skirt,
Platform sandals,
Tie-dyed T-shirt,
Bangles and beads,
And rings for my toes.
I'm glad my mom kept
All her great '60s clothes.

Martin Luther King, Jr. (April)
and Robert F. Kennedy (June)
are assassinated

Democratic National Headquarters
are burglarized
for political information

1968

1972

Vietnam

The questions linger on and on,
Who was right and who was wrong?
Why did we go, why did we fight?
Who was wrong and who was right?
Vietnam—to leave or stay?
To fight, to flee, or to obey?
The answers cloaked in shades of gray,
The questions never go away.

Watergate

Tricky Dick Nixon hired some spies,
Thought he would bug the other guys,
But he got caught, with no escape,
Trapped by his own recording tape.

Y2K

We're all prepared for Y2K,

Got firewood, water, and food stashed away.

At the stroke of midnight, there is no doubt,

The electrical power will surely go out.

Computers will crash, systems will fail,

No more phones, TV, or mail.

We'll grow our own food, live off the land,

Cook over a fire, sew clothes by hand.

You say it's past midnight

and everything's fine?

Well, um, er, ah,

then—never mind.

George W. Bush wins the 2000 election by 4 electoral votes;
loses the popular vote. R.B. Hayes wins 1876 electoral
election by 1 vote; loses the popular vote.

2000

Close Calls

Close Call I

The election was too close to call,

The count went on for days,

And, finally, a winner, by just one vote,

President Rutherford B. Hayes.

Close Call II

The election was too close to call,

Votes were counted, and counted anew,

The court stepped in, a winner declared.

The Prez? George Bush, number two.

PRESIDENTS ON PARADE
1945 Part IV

Truman stopped the buck,
Ike had general's stars,
Kennedy left too soon,
Johnson showed his scars.
Thirty-seven was Nixon,
Watergate did him in,
Ford was next, then Carter
With his famous grin.
Number forty, Reagan,
Star of movies and TV,
George Bush, the dad, was next,
"Please! No broccoli!"

Clinton at age 46,
Was number forty-two,
Followed by George W.,
And his cowboy crew.

Presidents marching
Down through the years,
To waves and hoorays
And boos and cheers.

**Nearly 3,000 are killed in terrorist attacks
on the World Trade Center, at the
Pentagon, and in the air over Pennsylvania**

September 11, 2001

The Lady

I know a lady, you might know her too,
She's seen a lot in her years.
Joyful reunions and sad good-byes,
Laughter, sighs, and tears.
She saw the towers' awful fall,
The smoke burned in her eyes.
She saw the fear and saw the grief,
The hope, the prayers, the cries.

And soon she saw the work begin,
A country unified,
She saw neighbor helping neighbor,
She saw a proud flag rise.
She saw it all from where she stands,
Beautiful and tall,
And still she holds her torch up high,
And still she welcomes all.

Title Index